Little Sticker Dolly Dressing
Summertime fairies

Written by Fiona Watt
Illustrated by Lizzie Mackay
Designed by Johanna Furst

T0371024

Contents

Flower meadow

Butterflies are fluttering and bees are buzzing as Honeydew and Marigold fly from flower to flower.

Use the stickers to dress the fairies, then decorate the pages.

Honeydew

Marigold

3

Hide-and-seek

Cowslip covers her eyes and starts
to count to twenty, as the fairies creep
away to hide amongst the trees.

Cowslip

Pippin

5

Daisy

Strawberry patch

Every summer, Daisy and Trixie search the woods for ripe, red strawberries. They pick the sweet berries and carefully put them into their little baskets to carry home.

Trixie

Rosa

Summer sunrise

As the first rays of sunshine light up the sky, fairies spread their wings and fly high above Fairyland. They twirl and flutter in the fresh morning air.

Jasmine

Sandy seashore

Waves roll gently onto the shore, as Nixie and Marin search for pretty seashells. They will take them home and use them to decorate their house and fairy garden.

Nixie

Marin

Fleur

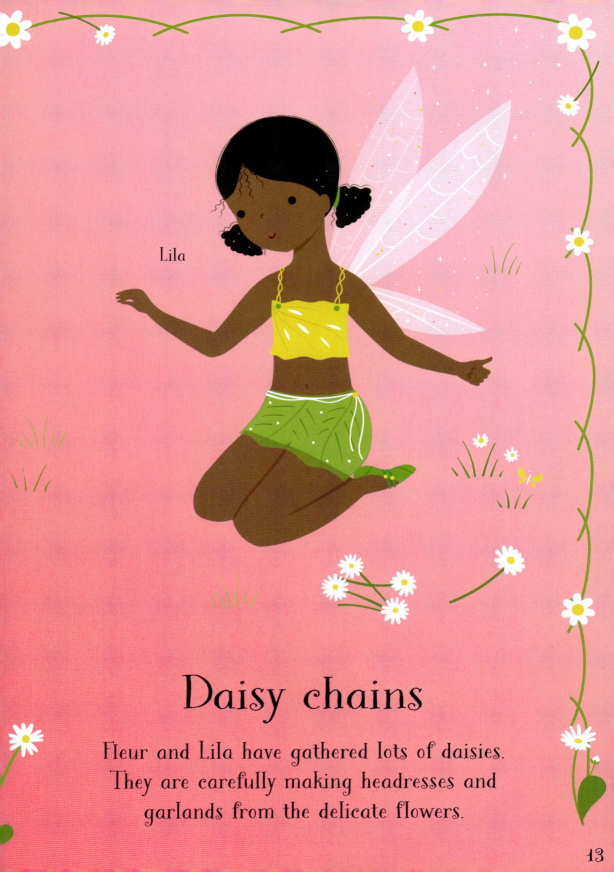

Lila

Daisy chains

Fleur and Lila have gathered lots of daisies.
They are carefully making headresses and
garlands from the delicate flowers.

Sundew

14

Sweetpea

Summer shower

A rainbow appears high in the sky, as raindrops pitter-patter to the ground. The fairies use big leaves to help them stay dry.

Faye

Flora

16

Midsummer dance

Flora, Faye and Candytuft have gathered flowers from the meadow to make garlands for their hair. They skip, dance and sing until the sun sets.

Candytuft

Picnic party

It's Willow's birthday and the fairies have invited their woodland friends to a picnic. They've made lots of delicious food for everyone to enjoy.

Willow

Cosmo

Elida

Water lily pond

On hot summer days, Elida and Posy love to
dip their toes into the cool water of the pond.
Dragonflies dart above them, while fish swim below.

Posy

21

Olwen

Rosehip

22

In the woods

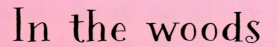

It's a very warm afternoon, too hot to be flying around Fairyland, so the fairies are keeping cool beneath the trees, as Nutmeg reads magical fairytales to Rosehip and Olwen.

Nutmeg

Twinkle

Stargazing

If Twinkle finds it difficult to sleep on warm summer nights, she loves to sit quietly watching the stars sparkling in the clear moonlit sky.

Flower meadow

Pages 2-3

Honeydew's headdress

Put Honeydew's skirt on before her top.

Marigold's headdress and dress

Hide-and-seek

Pages 4-5

Cowslip's headdress

Cowslip's skirt

Cowslip's shoes

Pippin's headdress

Pippin's outfit

Pippin's boots

Strawberry patch
Pages 6-7

Flowers for Daisy's hair

Daisy's outfit

Daisy's shoes

Trixie's headdress

Trixie's outfit

Summer sunrise
Pages 8-9

Rosa's headdress

Rosa's outfit

Jasmine's headdress and top

Jasmine's skirt

Sandy seashore
Pages 10-11

Nixie's headdress

Nixie's top and skirt

Decorations for Nixie's ankles

Marin's headdress

Marin's outfit

Daisy chains
Pages 12-13

Fleur's headdress

Fleur's skirt

Fleur's slippers

Lila's headdress and top

Lila's skirt

Summer shower
Pages 14–15

Sundew's headdress

Sundew's outfit

Sweetpea's outfit

Faye's dress

Midsummer dance
Pages 16–17

Flora's headdress

Candytuft's skirt

Flora's skirt

Picnic party
Pages 18-19

Willow's skirt

Willow's boots

Cosmo's headdress and outfit

Water lily pond
Pages 20-21

Elida's headdress

Elida's outfit

Flowers for Posy's hair

Posy's top and skirt

In the woods
Pages 22-23

Olwen's outfit

Flowers for Rosehip's hair

Nutmeg's headdress

Rosehip's clothes

Nutmeg's skirt and boots

Stargazing
Page 24

Twinkle's outfit

A flower for Twinkle's hair